GREEN SNAKE CEREMONY

Council Oak Publishing Co., Inc
1350 East 15th Street
Tulsa, OK 74120

First Edition
Printed in Hong Kong
99 98 97 96 95   5 4 3 2 1

Library of Congress Cataloging-in-Publication Data

Watkins, Sherrin, 1954–
    Green snake ceremony / by Sherrin Watkins ; illustrated by Kim Doner. — 1st ed.
       p.   cm. — (The Greyfeather series)
    Summary: As a young girl and her grandfather try to find the right kind of snake for a special
Shawnee ceremony, illustrations show what a nearby green snake thinks about everything.
    ISBN 0-933031-89-0 (cloth)
    1. Shawnee Indians—Rites and ceremonies—Juvenile fiction.
[1. Shawnee Indians—Rites and ceremonies—Fiction.   2. Indians of North America—Oklahoma—Fiction.
3. Snakes—Fiction.   4. Grandparents—fiction.]   I. Doner, Kim, 1955– ill. II. Title.
III. Series: Watkins, Sherrin, 1954– Greyfeather series.
PZ7.W315Gr   1995
[Fic]—dc20   95-37924
                                                                                                        CIP

                                                                                                        AC

ISBN 0-933031-89-0
ISBN 0-933031-26-2, *The Greyfeather Series*

GREEN SNAKE CEREMONY

by Sherrin Watkins
Illustrated by Kim Doner

Council Oak Books ◎ Tulsa Oklahoma
The Greyfeather Series

ary Greyfeather fidgeted, waiting for Grandma Greyfeather to be ready to go fishing. The noise of her cousins came through the open front door. A thud of the boys' feet on the porch boards made Mary jump.

"C'mon, Grandma!" they shouted.

Grandma was slow. She sat at her dinette table in front of a portable mirror, smoothing dark colored makeup over her broad face.

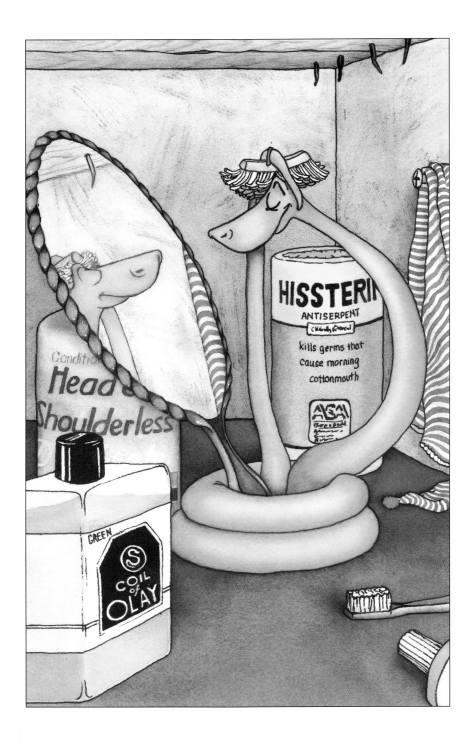

She talked to Mary. "I always catch the most fish because I take my time. I make myself presentable. If you were a fish, who would you prefer to be caught by — me or some child that leaves home looking like it hasn't combed its hair? Have you combed your hair today?" she asked.

Mary nodded "yes" at Grandma. Mary had been sorting through the quilt scraps which always sat on the table when Grandma and Grandpa weren't eating.

"Good! Fish like pretty things. I bet we catch the most fish."

"More than Grandpa?"

"I always catch more fish than Grandpa," Grandma said, her black eyes snapping with fun. "As I said, fish like pretty things."

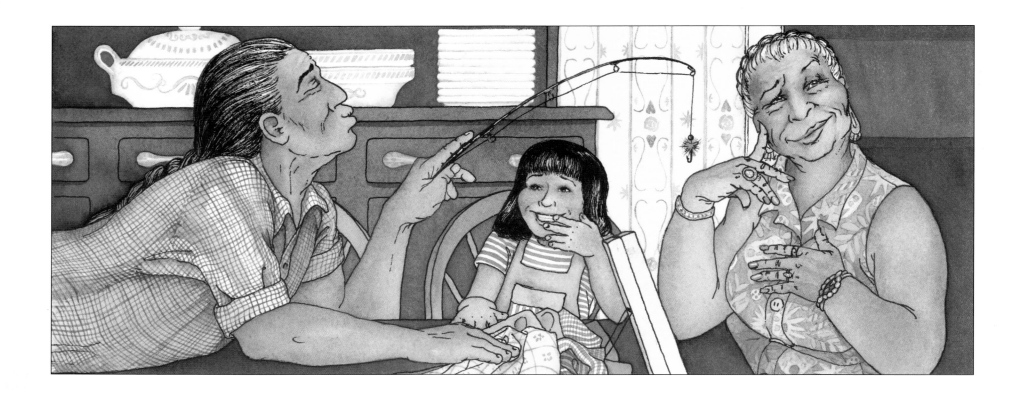

"That's why *I* always catch the most fish," said Grandpa Greyfeather, carrying fishing poles into the room. He winked at Mary.

"Hurry up, Esther," he said to Grandma. "Those boys will have the porch torn down if you get any prettier. They can help me look for a green snake today for Mary's green snake ceremony. That will keep them busy."

Mary asked, "What's a green snake ceremony?"

Her cousin Tony had been listening from the porch. "That's where they put a green snake in your mouth," he said. "Yum yum!"

Bobby joined in. "Boy, I'd sure hate to be that snake!"

"I'm afraid of snakes, Grandpa," Mary said. "Why do I have to have a snake in my mouth?"

"Green snakes won't hurt anyone, Mary. They're good luck, and they give girls your age good health," Grandpa said.

"They don't hurt little girls. Green snakes catch spiders and crickets and grasshoppers to eat, Wapapiyeshi," Grandma said, calling Mary by her Shawnee name and patting her hand.

Then Grandma went on to explain, "We put green snakes in the mouth of a child when she isn't a baby any more. Mary, you are old enough now to learn. You're going to begin school soon. You'll need the health and strength and luck a green snake will give you. That's why we do this for you."

    While Mary's grandma fished at Lake Yahola, Grandpa and Mary and her cousins
looked for a green snake.

    "They eat bugs," Grandpa told them, "and they like water." He showed them how to
look in the bushes and trees around Lake Yahola and in the surrounding Mohawk Park.

    "Why do we use a green snake instead of something else, Grandpa?" Mary's cousin,
Tony, asked.

    "Because it's our Shawnee belief," Grandpa said.

    "I think they're neat," said Tony.

    "Why is a snake healthy and good luck, Grandpa?" asked the twins.

    "Snakes are tough creatures," he said. "They are quiet and listen with their whole
bodies so they can learn and survive almost anything."

WELCOME!
To Oxley Nature
Center
Take Pictures—
Not Lives!

Afterwards, they went to Oxley Nature Center to hunt for a green snake. Here Mary learned that no one can hunt any kind of animal in a nature preserve.

Soon even Grandpa got tired of looking, and they returned to Lake Yahola.

"Well, Esther," he said to Grandma, "it looks like we'd better go to a pet store tomorrow." She nodded and added another fish to her stringer.

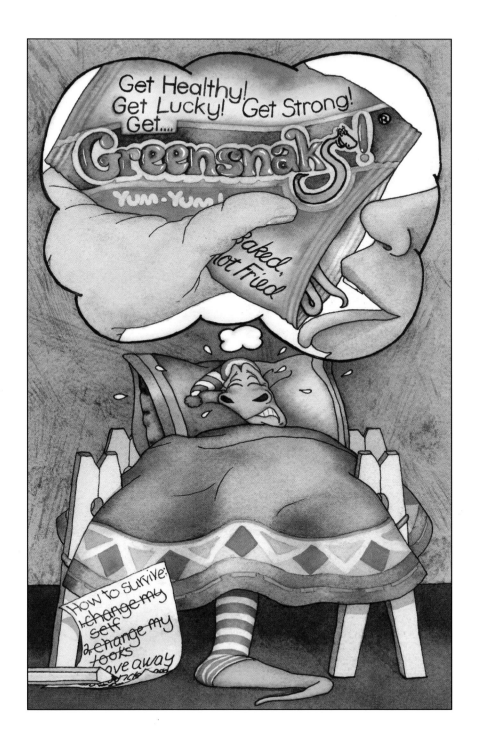

The next day Grandpa and Mary went to many pet stores, but no one had any green snakes. Mary saw beautiful fish, puppies, kittens, and even little garter snakes, but no green snakes.

"Next time I'll let my fingers do the walking," Grandpa told Mary as they were getting into the truck again. Then he stopped. He looked at Mary. "We're not going to find a green snake, Mary."

"How come?" she asked.

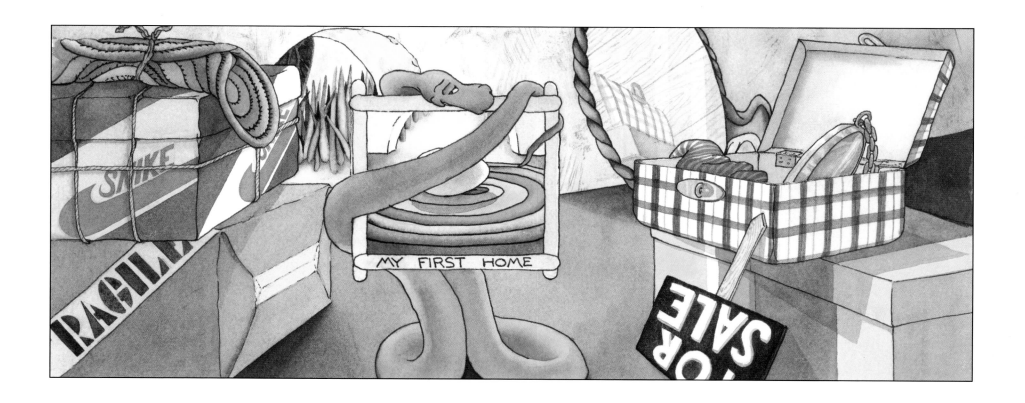

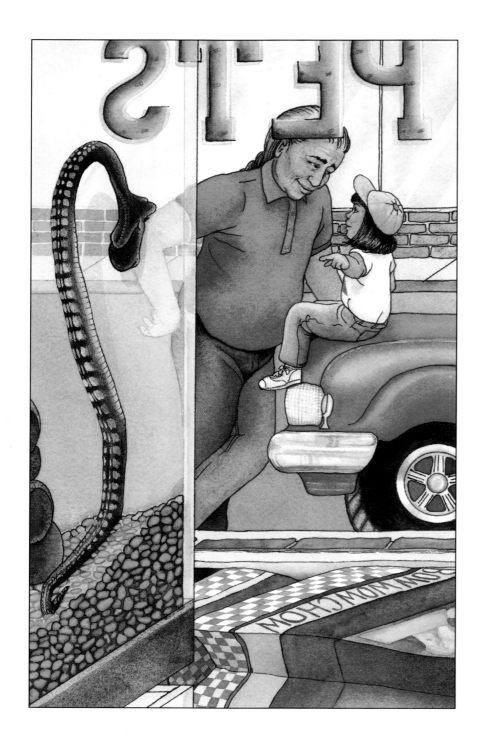

"Green snakes are wild snakes. They live near water where they can find food. Stores only sell tame snakes and, besides, I'm tired of snake hunting."

"Me, too," said Mary.

"Your folks will be here tonight to take you home. Let's just go back in there and get one of those little garter snakes."

"I liked that little one. Her name is Lillian."

"Lillian it is," he said.

They took the garter snake home.

That evening Mary's momma and dad came to get her. Her Grandma Spybuck was with them.

"Grandpa got us a pet snake named Lillian," Mary said, showing them the special aquarium and her snake.

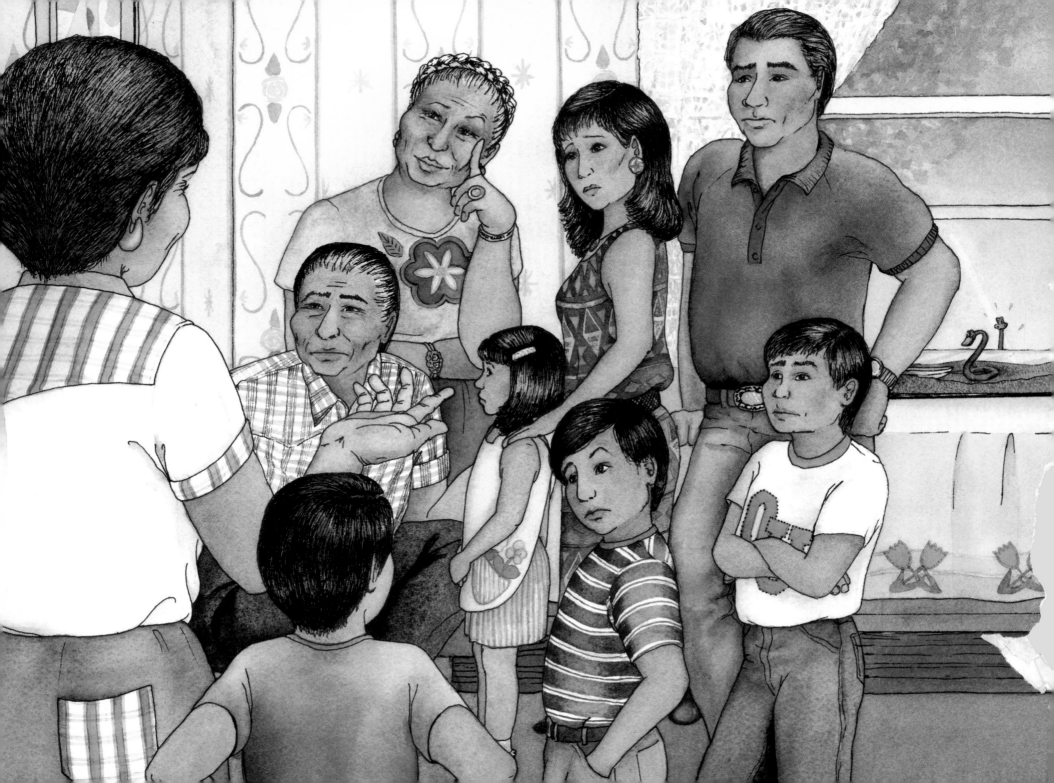

"Mary, Wapapiyeshi, *pialo*, come here," Grandpa said. "You're growing up. Old enough for school, old enough to learn."

Grandma added, "Because you're not a baby anymore we put this snake in your mouth, for good luck, good health."

"That's not a green snake," objected Grandma Spybuck. "Maybe the wrong kind of snake is bad luck."

"I couldn't find a green snake," said Grandpa.

"But what if it's bad luck to use anything but a green snake?" asked Mary's momma.

For a moment, no one knew quite what to do. Then Grandma Greyfeather grabbed her bag of quilt scraps, took a square of light green fabric and, reaching into the special aquarium, rolled it around Lillian's middle. "There!" she said, "a green snake!"

Grandpa asked, "Will it do in a pinch?"

Momma and Grandma Spybuck looked at each other for a moment and smiled. "It'll do in a pinch," said Grandma Spybuck, nodding.

Grandma Greyfeather held Lillian's head in one hand and her tail in the other. The green cloth wrapped Lillian from head to tail and made her look funny. Grandma turned to Mary.

"You're growing up," she said. "You've become old enough to learn and to mind your teachers." Mary opened her mouth and Grandma put the cloth-covered snake between Mary's lips for a second. "We now pray to God, *Maneto*, and ask that Mary, Wapapiyeshi, have good health and good fortune to take her through her life, to help her as she learns and grows."

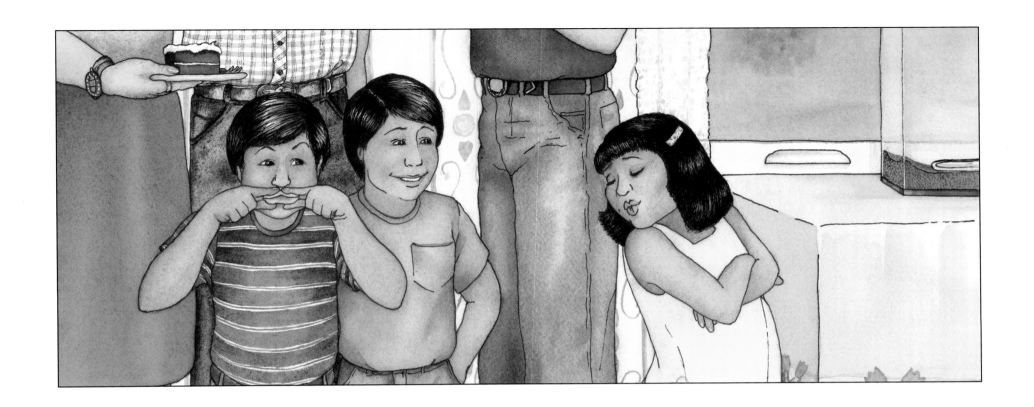

"Now you have snake lips," Bobby teased his cousin.

"Un-unh," said Mary. "Lillian had a cloth on her. I have cloth lips!"

"I'm just glad the women in this family sew," Mary's dad said to her.

"Me too," Mary nodded, tapping the side of Lillian's special aquarium as her grandma handed her a piece of cake that they had made for the celebration.

"What's going to happen to Lillian now, Grandpa?" asked Billy.

"I think we should just let her go," Grandpa replied.

"No," said Tony. "Someone might hurt her."

"I know!" said Mary. "Let's take Lillian to the Oxley Nature Preserve, where no one can hurt her!"

Grandpa smiled with pride. "I see our Mary is already listening and learning well. Oxley it is!"

Native American tribes share a deep respect for all animals and it shows in their history. Found throughout the teachings of storytellers are the Animal People: their strengths are admired and often serve as inspiring examples in many ceremonies.

The Shawnee people use the Green Snake to bless children as they begin growing up. Before modern times, life was much more dangerous. Strength, health, and luck, along with the abilities to stay quiet and listen well, were all important parts of surviving. Such traits are still found in this little reptile.

There are two kinds of Green Snakes in North America: the Smooth Green Snake and the Rough Green Snake. The Smooth Green Snake is also called the "green grass snake" and lives mostly on the ground. They eat spiders and insects. Their relative, the Rough Green Snake, is known as the "vine snake." A tree climber and swimmer, the vine snake often lives near a stream or lake. Their scales each have a thick, hard sort of bump called a "keel." These provide extra traction when they are climbing trees, making them the "rough" Green Snake. Both kinds of Green Snake are very, very gentle and should be treated that way. They only stay a beautiful green when they are alive; when they die, they turn a dull grey-blue.

JUST FOR FUN

Wild snakes are happier when left in the wild, but you might want to get a little "wild" about them. Draw your own snake character, then give him or her some personality! How many snake jokes can you come up with for your creation?

THINK ABOUT...

A favorite country/western song? (Achy Snakey Heart?)
A favorite ballad? (Greensleeveless?)
What sunglasses would one wear? (Snokeleys?)
Halloween costume? (Scaleton?)

Don't stop now! There's a "hole" world just waiting to be made!

MAKE A "WINDSNAKE"

Besides a grass snake or a vine snake, how about a wind snake? (Or maybe call it a windsnock?)

You will need: a small, clean margarine tub and top; a stapler or needle and thread or iron-on glue or superglue, ½ yard parachute fabric (maybe a bright green?); yellow, white and black felt; scissors, and string. A helpful grownup is also a big part of this project.

① First, cut the center from the top of the margarine bowl, leaving it a ½" ring. Next, cut the bottom half of the bottom, so there is about a 1" ring left there, too. This is the frame for the snock.

② Fold the material in half, lengthwise. Cut it at an angle, from the top corner to 3" at the bottom. Stitch, glue or staple it along the edges, leaving a hole at the top and bottom. Turn it right side out. Cut eyes, eyebrows and mouth. Stitch, staple or glue them about 10" from the top.

③ Gather a neck around the snock about 3" from the eyes. Stitch loosely, and leave a 3" circle there for the wind to blow through.

④ Open the plastic lids, and fold your snock inside. Add string. Snap the outside lid on, and hang him outside to show the direction the wind blows!